D0604993

SEE ME GO

Paul Meisel

NO LONGER PROPERTY
SEATTLE PUBLIC LIBRARY

I Like to Read®

HOLIDAY HOUSE • NEW YORK

I LIKE TO READ is a registered trademark of Holiday House Publishing, Inc.

Copyright © 2022 by Paul Meisel
All Rights Reserved
HOLIDAY HOUSE is registered in the U.S. Patent and Trademark Office.
Printed and bound in March 2022 at C&C Offset, Shenzhen, China.
The artwork was created with with pen and ink with watercolor and acrylic on Strathmore paper and digital tools.
www.holidayhouse.com
First Edition
1 3 5 7 9 10 8 6 4 2

This book has been officially leveled by using the F&P Text Level Gradient™ Leveling System.

Library of Congress Cataloging-in-Publication Data

Names: Meisel, Paul, author, illustrator.
Title: See me go / Paul Meisel.
Description: First edition. | New York : Holiday House, [2022]
Series: I like to read | Audience: Ages 4–8. | Audience: Grades K–1.
Summary: "Dozens of fun-loving dogs explore a sunken ship, take a rocket to the
moon, and visit an Egyptian tomb—where they are chased by
a giant cat"—Provided by publisher.
Identifiers: LCCN 2021040232 | ISBN 9780823444526 (hardcover)
Subjects: LCSH: Dogs—Juvenile fiction. | CYAC: Dogs—Fiction.
LCGFT: Picture books. | Readers (Publications)
Classification: LCC PZ7.M5158752 Sdp 2022 | DDC [E]—dc23
LC record available at https://lccn.loc.gov/2021040232

ISBN 978-0-8234-4452-6 (hardcover)

Here they come.

We jump on.

HI, DOG

We jump off.

We go down.

See us go.

We go, go, go!

We go out.

We go up.

We go up, up, up.

We go down.

We go down, down, down.

That is a very big cat.

Now we go again!

See me go.